MW00901233

THE BIRD AND THE WHALE

A Story of Unlikely Friendship

The Bird and the Whale
Emily Couture

Published by Couture Publishing

First Edition

HARDCOVER ISBN 978-1-7365234-0-7

Manufactured in North America.

TEXT | Emily Couture - www.CouturePublishing.com
ILLUSTRATION | Cathryn John - www.Flo-Studios.com
DESIGN & LAYOUT | Cathryn John - Flo. Studios

THE BIRD AND THE WHALE

Written by Emily Couture

Illustrated by Cathryn John

This book is dedicated to the littles in my life who've inspired me to make my dream a reality:

Addison, Carson, Christian, Evelyn, Frankie, Gabe, Harper, Isla, Josh, Liam, Lilah, Linc, Makenna, Zeke, Zia & Zöe.

And to my son, Rhett, who was born *just* in time to make the printing of this book. May you always be examples of the good that others seek in this world.

All my love,

Emily

On the sun-kissed surface of the water so deep
Is a place where the strangest of friends came to meet.

The bird and the whale did not understand
How one lived in water and the other on land.

Birds aren't like whales! (We all can agree.)
Have you seen a flying whale or a bird in the sea?

A bird has the freedom of infinite skies
While the whale swims deep down under the tides.

The whale was happy in his big ocean home
But he feared the skies and what was unknown.

The bird was so curious of Whale's life under water.
Did he know any mermaids? Had he met Mr. Otter?

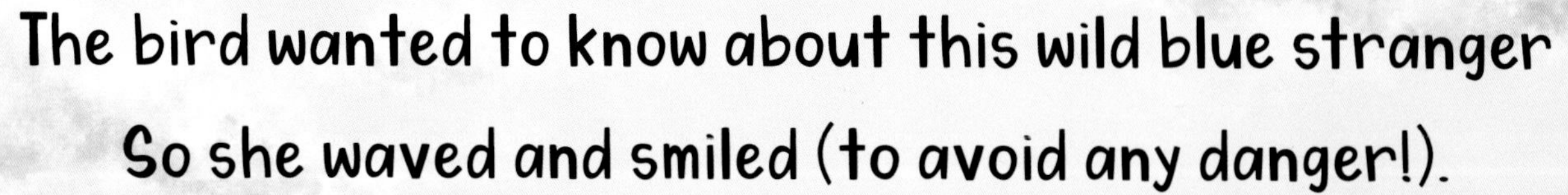

The bird wanted to know about this wild blue stranger
So she waved and smiled (to avoid any danger!).

Whale swam up to meet Bird on the surface
Though the idea of meeting new friends made him nervous.

"Our worlds are too different. We're nothing alike.
Where would we go? Whales can't take flight!"

But the more that they talked and the more Whale heard,

He saw his life really *was* like a bird's.

"You come to the surface to take a deep breath.
I come here for food, to cool off, and to rest.

Aren't fins just like wings with a layer of blubber?
I fly and you swim, one just like the other.

Maybe there's more to the middle, you see,
Than what makes us different, to you and to me.

Things can be different like the light and the dark
But to find common ground, we just look for a spark.

We both roam free in blue worlds of wonder.
We both seek shelter from the sky's rains and thunder."

The whale smiled and thought of the time he could spend

Talking and laughing with his new feathered friend.

On the surface is where the pair could now meet,

They'd watch the sun set and share fish to eat.

The bird tells the whale of her stories up high,
Of treetops and clouds and kites in the sky.

The whale tells his tales of shipwrecks and treasure
And creatures from water that's too deep to measure.

There is something so special about meeting a friend
And finding your differences don't matter much in the end.

The whale learned that flying wasn't far from his reach

And with his big fins, shot up with a breach.

For those few moments of air, he felt like a bird
And they smiled together without saying a word.

There's beauty in different, the odd and unknown.
Meeting new friends means we're never alone.